# This book belongs to:

_____

_____

# Test Your Colors Here

# Country Hayride

# At home in the sea

heart

spoon

ring

banana

snail

open book

high-heeled shoe

eagle's head

lizard

goose

toucan

Humpty Dumpty's head

spectacles

dog

Find the hidden objects

Find the hidden objects

ENVELOPE   PENCIL   BIRD   SHOE   BALL

CROWN   BOOMERANG   PEAR   CANDY   CANDLE   BALLOON   HORSESHOE   FLAG   TEPEES

Find the hidden objects

Find the hidden objects

Find the hidden objects

Find the hidden objects

eyeglasses

crown

pencil

feather

bell

bird

glove

paper clip

ring

fish

mushroom

dress

heart

squirrel

spoon

ice-cream
cone

FLASHLIGHT
CROWN
CATERPILLAR
CONES
MOUSE
CORN
DIAMOND
CAR
BIRD
CARROT
BALLOON
CHERRY
PLUNGER
FOOTBALL
TEPEES(2)
ORNAMENT

# Three Little Pigs Hidden Objects

Can you find the 15 hidden items?

domino

snail

mountains

seahorse

boot

pizza

ufo

candle

watch

envelope

crown

heart

baseball bat

brush

fish

artist's brush

cap

saw

spectacles

crescent moon

sailing boat

tortoise

iron

mitten

shoe

candle

ice lolly

mug

# Hidden Pictures

Find the hidden objects

Made in United States
Troutdale, OR
01/19/2024

17024420R00031